Can you?

Written by Hatty Skinner
Illustrated by Rotem Teplow

Collins

It can quack and honk.

Can you?

It can zip and buzz.

Can you?

It can yap and wag.

Can you?

It can hang.

Can you?

web

It can dash.

Can you? Quick!

It can zigzag.

Can you?

fangs

/j/

14

/ch/

After reading

Letters and Sounds: Phase 3

Word count: 39

Focus phonemes: /j/ /w/ /y/ /z/ zz /qu/ /sh/ /ng/ /nk/

Common exception words: you, and

Curriculum links: Understanding the world; Physical development

Early learning goals: Reading: read and understand simple sentences; use phonic knowledge to decode regular words and read them aloud accurately; read some common irregular words

Developing fluency

- Your child may enjoy hearing you read the book.
- Take turns to read to a double page, encouraging your child to read the questions expressively. Encourage your child to read the labels, too.

Phonic practice

- Ask your child to sound out and blend these words:

  z/i/p   b/u/zz   qu/i/ck   d/a/sh   z/i/g/z/a/g

- Turn to page 13 and point to the label. Ask your child to read the word and find the two letters that together make one sound. (f/a/**ng**/s)
- Look at the "I spy sounds" pages (14–15) together. Point to and sound out the the /j/ and /ch/.
  Say: I spy a /ch/ in "cheetah" and point to the cheetah. Say: I spy a /j/ in "jeep" and point to the jeep. Encourage your child to do the same, finding /j/ and /ch/ things (or actions) in the picture. (e.g. *chase, chair, chicks, ostrich, watch, jump, jet, jeans, jewellery, jacket*)

Extending vocabulary

- Focus on the meanings of **yap** and **fangs**. Ask your child:
  - Does **yap** mean exactly the same as bark or is it a bit different? (e.g. *a yap is a small bark or a puppy's bark*)
  - Does **fangs** mean exactly the same as teeth or is it a bit different? (e.g. *fangs are very sharp pointed teeth*)